Veronika Martenova Charles

Illustrated by David Parkins

TUNDRA BOOKS

Published in Canada by Tundra Books,
75 Sherbourne Street, Toronto, Ontario M5A 2P9

Published in the United States by Tundra Books of Northern New York,
P.O. Box 1030, Plattsburgh, New York 12901

Library of Congress Control Number: 2009938095

Library and Archives Canada Cataloguing in Publication

Charles, Veronika Martenova
       It's not about the crumbs! / Veronika Martenova
Charles ; illustrated by David Parkins.

(Easy-to-read wonder tales)
ISBN 978-0-88776-953-5

       1. Fairy tales. 2. Children's stories, Canadian (English).
I. Parkins, David II. Title. III. Series: Charles, Veronika
Martenova. Easy-to-read wonder tales.

PS8555.H42242I872 2010   jC813'.54   C2009-905858-8

We acknowledge the financial support of the Government of Canada through
the Book Publishing Industry Development Program (BPIDP) and that of the
Government of Ontario through the Ontario Media Development Corporation's
Ontario Book Initiative. We further acknowledge the support of the Canada Council
for the Arts and the Ontario Arts Council for our publishing program.

ONTARIO ARTS COUNCIL
CONSEIL DES ARTS DE L'ONTARIO

Printed and bound in Canada

1 2 3 4 5 6   15 14 13 12 11 10

CONTENTS

POPCORN
PART 1

On Saturday, Jake's mother said,

"We're going to visit Uncle Mike

at his new house.

I have to help him unpack."

"Can Lily and Ben come?"

asked Jake.

"Okay," Jake's mom replied.

"There is a park near the house

where you can play."

"How do we get to the park?"

asked Jake, when they arrived.

"It's easy," said Uncle Mike.

"Go left at the end of the street,

walk two blocks, and turn right."

Jake grabbed a bag of popcorn,

then he, Lily, and Ben took off.

When they turned the corner,

Jake opened the bag,

and began to drop popcorn

on the ground.

"What are you doing?" asked Lily.

"I'm leaving a trail so we can

find the way back," said Jake.

"I get it," said Ben,

"like in Hansel and Gretel."

"But didn't they use crumbs?"

asked Lily.

"In the story I know," said Jake,

they used corn to mark the trail."

Jake, Lily, and Ben found the park

and sat down on the grass.

"Tell us that story," said Ben.

"Okay," said Jake.

7

THE CHILDREN IN THE WOODS

(*Hansel and Gretel* from Europe)

There was a man and woman

who had two children

called Marek and Jana.

One night, the woman

told her husband,

"There is nothing left to eat.

I can no longer feed our children.

Tomorrow you must take them

and lose them in the woods.

Surely someone will find them

and take care of them."

Marek was not asleep.

He heard everything

and saw his mother crying.

In the morning, the father said,

"Get ready children, we are going

to gather some firewood."

Before they left, Marek found

a few dry corncobs in the house

and hid them under his shirt.

On the way through the woods,

Marek began to drop the corn.

Deep in the forest,

the father said, "Wait here.

I will look for wood nearby."

And he went away.

Marek and Jana waited for hours.

"I don't think Father is coming,"

Marek said to his sister.

"But don't worry. I can find

our way back home."

Marek tried to follow his trail,

but birds had eaten the corn.

It was getting dark. The children

walked through the woods

until they came to a rock cliff.

From there, they saw a light

on the far side of the valley.

They headed toward the light

and came to a small road

that led them to a house.

The children knocked on the door.

An old woman opened it

and told them to come in.

Inside, there was a small girl,

the same age as Marek and Jana.

She brought dinner to the table.

When Marek looked at his food,

there seemed to be a finger

sticking out of it!

"Don't eat it!" he warned Jana.

The children excused themselves,

climbed up to the attic,

and went to sleep.

Now, the old woman,

who was a witch, had a plan.

After the children left the table,

she told Blanka, her servant girl,

"More for the pot!

What a good stew they will make!

Before the sun comes up,

wake me, and I will kill them."

The witch went to bed.

But poor Blanka

began to wonder

just how safe *she* was

from day to day.

Could she save these children

and save herself too?

Maybe the magic she'd learned

from spying on the witch

could help them all escape.

When the witch was sound asleep,

Blanka climbed into the attic.

"Wake up!" she whispered

to Marek and Jana.

"The witch is going to cook you.

You must get away from here!"

19

The children crept downstairs.

Blanka spat on the door, and then

all three children ran out.

The noise of the door closing

woke up the witch.

"Is it morning yet?" she called.

And the spit on the door answered,

"Not yet. You can still sleep.

I'll make a cooking fire."

The witch went back to sleep,

but in a while, she woke again.

"Is the fire ready yet?"

Again, the spit answered,

"The wood was damp. Go to sleep!"

Then, the sun came up.

The witch jumped up and yelled,

"You lazybones, where are you?"

This time there was no answer,

because the sun had dried up

the spit on the door.

The witch saw there was no fire,

and all the children were gone.

She went out and sniffed around

until she smelled which way

they had gone.

Then, she set off after them.

The children reached the big cliff

and found a cave under it

just wide enough to crawl into.

They slipped in there and hid.

Soon the witch found them.

She tried to squeeze in

to grab them, but she couldn't.

Never mind, the witch thought.

They'll get hungry in a few days.

She waited on the rock cliff,

but by and by, she fell asleep.

The children heard her snoring.

They crept up behind the witch

and gave her a hard push.

The witch rolled down the cliff,

broke her bones, and died.

Marek and Jana found their house,

and Blanka returned

to her own home

and was welcomed by her family.

"This reminds me of another story

about kids who are lost

and come to the house

of a cannibal woman," said Lily.

"These kids ran away from home,

so they didn't need corn

to mark their way back."

"What happened to them?"

asked Jake.

"I will tell you," said Lily.

ZAHRA AND BINTI

(*Hansel and Gretel* from Africa)

Zahra and Binti were sisters.

They lived with their father

in a village on the River Nile.

Once their father went away

and left them with his relatives

who were cruel and beat them.

"We have to run away!"

Zahra said to Binti.

The next day, the sisters left

and walked until evening came.

Far off, they saw two fires,

a big one and a little one.

"Let's go to the big fire,"

said Binti.

They came to a house in the desert.

A gigantic woman with large teeth

and red eyes came from inside.

"Welcome!" she greeted the girls.

She invited them to eat with her

and spend the night in her house.

After they had eaten,

Zahra and Binti went to bed,

but they couldn't sleep.

They heard the sound of metal

scraping against a rock

and the woman singing:

"Rock is smooth, rock is hard,

and it makes my dull ax sharp."

The sisters were frightened,

and Binti cried out.

"What's the matter?"

the woman asked.

"We can't sleep," Zahra answered.

"The camels are keeping us awake."

The woman left her house

and walked to the little fire

to talk to the camel owners.

"You there!" she called out.

"Move your camels out of here!"

33

But as soon as the woman left,

Zahra and Binti jumped

out of their bed,

put rocks under the blanket,

and ran away from the house.

34

When the woman returned,

she picked up her ax and swung it

at the two bumps in the bed.

Clang, clang!

The ax made a sound

as it hit the rocks.

The woman screamed in rage.

She ran after the girls.

Soon, Zahra and Binti saw

a cloud of dust behind them.

The woman was chasing them.

The girls came to a wide river.

A crocodile was swimming there.

"Please crocodile," Zahra called,

"take us to the other side!"

"I will eat you up!"

the crocodile answered.

"If you take us, I promise you

a bigger dinner," Zahra yelled.

So the crocodile took them across.

Soon, the gigantic woman arrived

on the other riverbank.

Zahra said to the crocodile,

"Go back and bring our auntie."

The crocodile went back

and the woman jumped on his back.

When he was halfway across,

Zahra shouted, "Crocodile!

Your dinner is on your back!"

Splash! The crocodile dove,

turned under the water,

and ate the woman up.

Zahra and Binti went back

to the village and arrived

just as their father returned.

Lily got up and went toward

the playground.

"I'm going to climb the dinosaur,"

she said.

"He looks like a crocodile."

Ben and Jake followed her.

"I also know a story about kids

who come to the house of a giant

who eats people," said Ben.

"Does the giant eat them up?"

asked Jake.

"I'll tell the story," said Ben.

THE OGRE

(*Hansel and Gretel* from Japan)

There was once a woman

who had three sons.

Since her husband died,

she'd worked hard to feed them,

but they were often hungry.

I can't let my children suffer,

she thought.

I will take them to the mountains

and leave them there.

If they die of the cold, at least

it will be faster than starving.

So, the woman took her sons

high into the mountains.

"Wait here," she told the boys.

"I'm going to get you some food."

Then she left them there

and returned home.

The boys waited until dark.

When their mother didn't return,

the two older boys began to cry.

"Crying won't do any good,"

said Kenji, the youngest one.

"I'll climb a tree and search for

a place where we can stay."

From high in the tree,

Kenji saw a light in the distance.

"Let's go to it,"

he called to his brothers

and showed them which way to go.

At last, they came to a hut.

There was an old woman inside,

sitting by the fire.

The boys entered the house.

"We are lost and can't find

our way in the dark.

May we stay here tonight?"

"I would like to help you,"

the woman replied,

"but this is an ogre's house.

The ogre will be home soon.

If he finds you, he will eat you.

You should leave right now."

As she was talking, they heard

the ogre's footsteps outside.

THUMP, THUMP.

"I told you!" the woman cried.

"Hurry, hide in here."

She put them in a storage pit

and covered it with a mat.

Just then, the ogre came in.

Sniff, sniff, he smelled the air.

"It stinks of humans," he said

and began to search the hut.

The old woman was frightened.

"A while ago three boys came by.

Then they ran away," she said.

"Their odor must still be here."

"Maybe I can still catch them,"

said the ogre.

He put on his *hundred mile* boots

and shot away like an arrow.

He ran far, but didn't find them.

Perhaps I went too *far,* he thought.

The boys will surely come soon.

He sat down and fell asleep.

When the ogre left, the woman

opened up the storage pit.

"The ogre had his fast boots on.

He will be far away by now,"

she told the boys.

"Run for your lives!"

The boys hurried along the path

until they heard thunder.

Wondering what it was,

they went closer and saw the ogre

snoring by the road.

The two older boys were so scared

that they started to cry.

"Crying won't do any good,"

Kenji told his brothers.

"If we can get the ogre's boots,

he won't be able to catch us."

Kenji snuck up to the ogre

and gently pulled his boots off,

one by one.

He took them to his brothers.

"Put them on!" he told them,

giving each brother one boot.

"Now, fly!" said Kenji

and he held onto his brothers.

Instantly they flew into the air.

Soon they saw their mother's house

and they landed on the ground.

Their mother was glad to see them,

and her sons worked hard,

using the magical boots

to help earn money for food.

★ ★ ★

POPCORN
PART 2

"Let's go back and see

if the popcorn is still there,"

Jake said to Ben and Lily.

"In *Hansel and Gretel*,

the crumbs get eaten by birds,"

said Lily.

As they walked back,

they found the popcorn

still on the ground.

Lily and Ben chased after it.

"I guess there are not many birds

around here," said Lily.

"Maybe they don't like popcorn,"

said Ben.

The three kids turned the corner.

"This is the street," said Jake.

"Which house is your uncle's?"

asked Ben.

"They all look the same."

"I don't know," answered Jake.

"I didn't look at the number."

"We'll have to wait," said Lily.

They sat down on the curb.

Finally, a door opened,

and Jake's mother came out.

"I was just about to go

and look for you," she said.

"I thought maybe you got lost."

"We came back a while ago,"

said Lily.

"Mom, do you have more popcorn?"

Jake asked. "We're starving."

"I can make you some," she said,

and they all went inside.

ABOUT THE STORIES

The Grimms' story of *Hansel and Gretel* is perhaps the most popular of tales about small children who outsmart a witch or an ogre. But there are many other stories of this type, told in different cultures.

The Children in the Woods is based in part on an American-English folktale, *The Two Lost Babes*. Here I have combined it with a few other elements from similar European tales.

Zahra and Binti has its roots in several versions of a story called *Fatma the Beautiful*, that comes from the Nubian culture in Sudan, Africa.

The Ogre is based on the story called *The Oni and the Three Children* that is widespread in Japan.